DINOSAUR FARM!

KU-175-236

Triceratops

Allosaurus

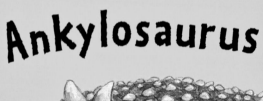

Ankylosaurus

Iguanodon

Carnotaurus

Megalosaurus

Stegosaurus

Baryonyx

Styracosaurus

Tyrannosaurus
rex

For Lucia

First published 2019 by Nosy Crow Ltd
The Crow's Nest, 14 Baden Place
Crosby Row, London SE1 1YW
www.nosycrow.com

ISBN 978 1 78800 180 9 (HB)
ISBN 978 1 78800 181 6 (PB)

Nosy Crow and associated logos are trademarks
and/or registered trademarks of Nosy Crow Ltd.

Text and illustrations copyright © Penny Dale 2019

The right of Penny Dale to be identified as the author
and illustrator of this work has been asserted.

All rights reserved

This book is sold subject to the condition that it shall not, by way of trade or otherwise, be lent,
hired out or otherwise circulated in any form of binding or cover other than that in which
it is published. No part of this publication may be reproduced, stored in a retrieval system,
or transmitted in any form or by any means (electronic, mechanical, photocopying,
recording or otherwise) without the prior written permission of Nosy Crow Ltd.

A CIP catalogue record for this book is available from the British Library.

Printed in China

Papers used by Nosy Crow are made from wood grown in sustainable forests.

1 3 5 7 9 8 6 4 2 (HB)
1 3 5 7 9 8 6 4 2 (PB)

DINOSAUR FARM!

Penny Dale

nosy crow

Farmer dinosaurs **working,**
working on Dinosaur Farm.

Driver dinosaurs ploughing, ploughing the stony soil.
The stony soil, row after row.

Up and down!
Up and down!
Up and down!

Shepherd dinosaur zooming,
zooming over the hills.
Over the hills, to feed the sheep.

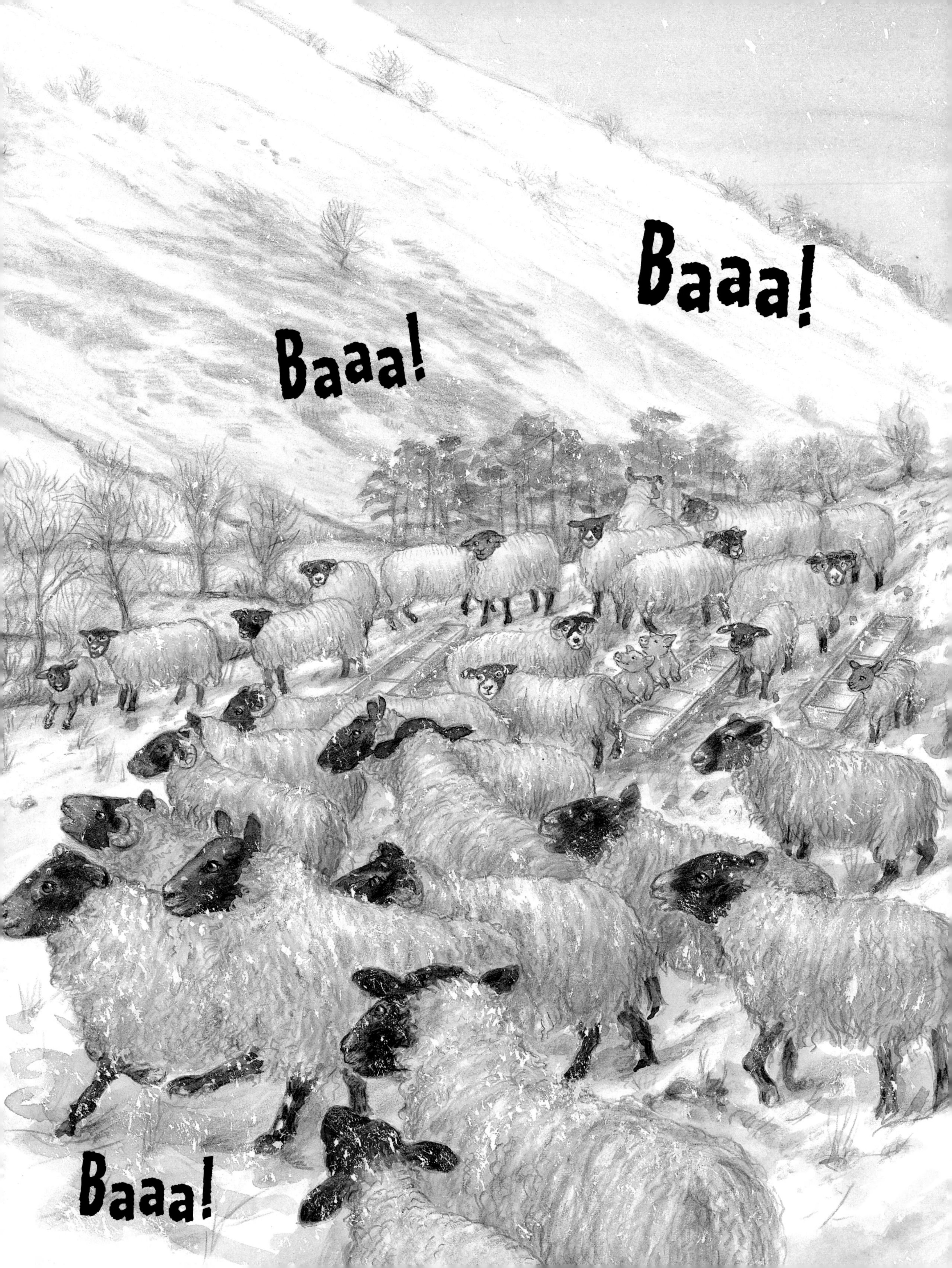
Baaa!
Baaa!
Baaa!

Smelly dinosaur muck-spreading,
muck-spreading across the field.

Across the field, feeding the soil.

Splatter!

Splatter! Splatter!

Haymaking dinosaurs rolling,
rolling up the long grass.
The long grass into giant bales!

Thud!

Thud!

Thud!

Dusty dinosaurs digging,
digging the muddy carrots.

Clatter!

The muddy carrots to be
washed and stacked.
Clatter!

Clatter!

Rumble!

Sunny dinosaurs cutting,
cutting the golden corn.

The golden corn with the
combine harvester.

Rumble!

Rumble!

Climbing dinosaurs picking, picking the juicy red apples.

Excited dinosaurs travelling, travelling to the **farm show.**

To the **farm show** with their **animals** and **crops**.

Chatter!

Chatter!

Chatter!

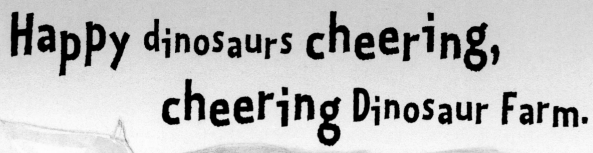

Happy dinosaurs cheering,
cheering Dinosaur Farm.

Carrot picker

Quad bike

Tractor and plough

Combine harvester

Muck spreader

Animal
transporter

Apple
picker

Fence post
driver

Hay
baler